It is a time of terror, wonder, and pleasures undreamed of. The gods are dead and the great demons gnaw at their bones. From the cannibal kingdom of Kaszanka to the sordid pornocracy of Thune, life is frenzied and cheap. Fortunes and kingdoms are bartered at the swing of a blade. Lawlessness and lust rule the day, while magic and mayhem take charge of the night. Slavery and massacre swarm across the land like ants at a picnic, while notes of demon laughter dance over all like shadows of flames from the deific pyre. It is the Aeon of Chaos, and only Chaos reigns!

Also by B.J. Swann

Aeon of Chaos Novels
Zhuulton of Zhuul and the Feast of the Centipede
Zhuulton of Zhuul and the Conspiracy of Ravens

Aeon of Chaos Novellas
The Court of the Mushroom King
The Crimson Crown
The Unwithering Flower

Aeon of Chaos Short Stories
The Bone House
The Lovers in Flame
The Magickal Goat Boy
The Second Wolf

Novels
Baron Bad Trip
Our Lady of the Scythe

With Elizabeth Bedlam
Holocaust Hearts
Temperance Holocaust

Narseh the Slayer and the Lucre of Death

An Aeon of Chaos Novelette

By B.J. Swann

Contents

Chapter 1: Among the Tombstones

It's the Aeon of Chaos. The gods are dead, and the demons roll marbles made from their eyes.

Narseh the slaver strolled through the graveyard with a bouquet of flowers in hand. He glanced at the gravestones as he walked. Many were corroded with age. Some had collapsed into piles of dirty rubble. Those still standing bore laconic and sinister epitaphs. One simply said 'here I lie; soon you shall join me.' Another catalogued the impressive career of a local magistrate, whose *curriculum vitae* ended with a description of his current occupation: 'worm food.'

Narseh held back a shudder. Like most people he didn't like to think about mortality, and harboured a natural terror of death. But even greater than his fear of dying was his fear of dying before he became outrageously and fabulously wealthy.

People often said 'you can't take money with you

when you die.' Narseh knew them to be fools. For he had consulted with certain experts regarding the transmigration of souls and the mysterious realm of the underworld. From them he had purchased the rituals which would allow him to transplant his wealth into the afterlife when the time of his death arrived.

He had the whole thing planned out. As soon as he died, all his worldly assets would be liquidated into gold, jewels, silks and tobacco, then placed inside a giant magickal circle. From there they would be teleported into the realm of the dead, where his soul would be waiting to collect the cache. He wouldn't have to carry all that loot by himself; he'd left detailed instructions for his wives and slaves to kill themselves the moment he died, so that they too might continue to serve him in the afterlife. And in the event that they should demur from such a morbid request, and linger on beyond him in the realm of the living, he had placed some assassins on retainer to garrotte them.

Thus Narseh hoped to retire to the afterlife in fabulous style. The problem was he just didn't have enough money yet. He was rich, to be sure – but not rich enough to sustain himself throughout the long, untold aeons he might end up spending in the underworld.

His anxiety deepened as he walked among the tombstones in the wealthier section of the graveyard. Most were decorated with statues of the morbid demons who dwelt in the lands of the dead. Most commonly depicted was the Lady of the Scythe, a terrible and beautiful figure who stood with her eponymous weapon raised above her head. She was always shown naked, save for a belt from which tiny human beings hung on hooks like the strips of a revealing leather skirt. Her statues were smeared with ritual ashes, for her true physical body was said to have congealed from the countless cremains of a gigantic funeral pyre.

It was demons like her, Narseh had been told, whom he would have to bribe in order to secure safe passage and fine accommodation in the underworld. Because the underworld, apparently, was much like the realm of the living – a chaotic, greedy place in which there were all sorts of people who needed to be bribed. Local warlords, ferrymen, demons – the list was endless! Who knew how much money they'd ask for? If Narseh wasn't careful, he'd end up spending most of his resources just paying them off. And if he didn't accumulate enough capital before that fateful day, he might end up just another member of the deceased bourgeoisie, condemned to a droll eternity. Even worse – he might end up a pauper, with hardly two sticks of gold to rub together!

The very thought was almost enough to make him tear out his beard in terror. He had to secure his great nest egg before it was too late. Feeling the presence of death all around him, standing in the shadow of the Lady's wicked scythe, he offered up a prayer to the Candle King.

'Oh great Candle King,' said Narseh. 'Please don't let me die yet. Don't snuff out my life – not until I'm fabulously rich! I'll garland your altars with gold if you just let me live until then!'

Narseh fell silent, waiting for some sign the Candle King had heard him. There came only the rustling of wind through graveside weeds. Narseh took that as a positive sign, and quelled his anxiety. Besides, he didn't have time to be worrying about mortality – he was here to make money.

With a renewed sense of purpose he strode through the cemetery, peering at the gravestones as he went, as though he were searching for a specific grave. In truth, he was searching for a funeral service he knew to be taking place that afternoon.

He came upon it soon enough. There, in the wealthiest section of the graveyard, was a freshly dug grave with casket in place. A small group of people stood gathered around it: a pair of dirty gravediggers, a rite master, and a middle-aged woman in luxurious attire. The latter was the wife and only heir of the dead man, one Kinevel Kruze. The widow sobbed, wiping her eyes with a handkerchief. Her grief was very fresh, for her husband had died only one day before. The speed of his burial might have seemed unusual in other lands, but here in the province of Hillshadow such practices were standard, for ancient tradition demanded the dead be inhumed within twenty-four hours, lest their souls grow attached to the landscape and torment the living.

Narseh knew all of these details from his careful research. Allowing a brief and sinister smile to flash unseen across his lips, the slaver knelt before a random grave in close proximity to the funeral. Pretending to pay his respects, he placed his bouquet of flowers on the grave and composed his face into a sorrowful mask.

'Oh my dear long-lost cousin,' he said dramatically, before pausing to scan the name of the deceased, which he hadn't yet looked at.

'Oh fuck,' he hissed.

The dead man's name was not 'Fuck,' of course; it was Paerulicent Amberkance Perfleeticat the Third. A ridiculous name which Narseh would now have to remember and recite in order to maintain his deception. He sighed, wishing he'd taken more time to scan the writing on the tombstones.

Too late now, he thought, and continued to address the dead stranger in tones both dramatic and doleful.

'Oh my dear long-lost cousin, Paerulicent Amberkance Perfleeticat the Third. Such a tragedy I never got to know you. So sad we were separated by the wide Ozich Sea. Still, I'm glad I can offer you these flowers. Perhaps they'll bring you some comfort, down there in the underworld...'

'Though not for long,' he whispered. 'Since I'm going to steal them right back!'

Narseh chuckled under his breath, then wondered again about the strange economics of the Underworld. Would the dead Paerulicent receive the bouquet in the afterlife, only for the flowers to vanish from his hands the moment they were stolen back from the grave? Or would they remain with him forever, transfigured into roses for the dead?

The wailing of the widow roused Narseh from his musings. Her cries were followed by the droning of the rite master as he called upon the great cosmic demons to please watch over the deceased – and to please refrain from eating his soul. Soon the gravediggers were shovelling earth atop the casket while the still-weeping widow was consoled by the celebrant. One by one the clods fell, until the grave was filled with wet, bulging dirt. The diggers tamped it down with the backs of their spades, then bowed to the widow and departed in silence. For a time she remained there, wiping her tears and peering at the grave, till the rite master placed a comforting hand upon her shoulder and led her away toward the cemetery gates.

Narseh remained on his knees, waiting, feeling a pulse of excitement within.

The moment is at hand!

No sooner had those thoughts passed through his head than a muffled sound arose from the ground, as of someone beating a fist against the sealed coffin lid.

Chapter 2: The Second Death

Narseh raced to the freshly-filled grave and fell to his knees beside it. Gritting his teeth, he plunged his manicured hands into the soil, clawing it towards him.

How utterly repulsive, he thought. Not only was he pawing at the worm-laden soil of a grave, even worse – he was performing manual labour!

Such work was for underlings and slaves, not a well-bred merchant such as he. And yet, for his deception to work, he would have to get his hands dirty – at least a little. He swallowed his pride, thinking of the wealth he would receive if all went to plan. The thoughts washed away his unease. For Narseh the slaver would swim through a sewer if a pile of gleaming gold were at the end of it.

He continued to dig, while the muted sound of hammering continued to arise from below, sounding more and more desperate with each passing moment.

'Help!' shouted Narseh. 'Somebody help!'

The two gravediggers rushed into view, still carrying their shovels.

'Hey!' shouted one of them. 'What's all this carrying on?'

'Someone's alive down there,' said Narseh. 'Listen!'

Narseh suspended his digging, while the gravediggers bent their dirty ears toward the sounds from below. Loose soil quivered as the body in the casket beat upon the lid.

'Butcher's balls!' shouted one of the gravediggers, while the other remained frozen in shock.

'Start digging you idiots,' shouted Narseh, 'before the poor man runs out of air!'

The gravediggers hefted their spades and dug like madmen. Narseh stepped back, cleaning his hands with a silken kerchief, avoiding the soil as it flew from their shovels. Messy mounds of earth rose up beside the grave, while the thudding from the casket grew louder and louder, accompanied by terrified cries from within. The diggers worked harder as they heard those fearful shouts, sweating and grunting from their efforts, till their shovels slammed hard against the coffin's naked timber. Tossing their shovels by the graveside, they knelt in the pit and pried off the lid.

The figure within was bloated and pale; from his flesh came a whiff of decay. He sat up at once, panting, glancing around.

'It's about bloody time,' he said. 'I very nearly died in there!'

'We thought you were dead,' said one of the grave-diggers. 'That's why we buried you! If this man over here hadn't heard you...' he gestured to Narseh, who stood at the edge of the grave looking down.

'So this is my saviour,' said the man in the casket. 'Help me up, will you?'

He reached out with a pale, puffy hand. Narseh knelt and helped him out of the grave, feeling the hackles on his neck stiffen as he did so. Touching that flesh was even worse than touching the grave dirt – even worse than his short stint of manual labour! And yet, it was a necessary sacrifice for the riches to come.

Finally the dead man stood up beside the grave, shooting Narseh a gratified smile.

'Thank you, kind sir,' he said. 'I'm not sure I can ever repay you, but I'm going to try all the same. If it wasn't for you, I'd have died in that horrible hole!'

'Actually,' said Narseh, gesturing to the gravediggers with feigned humility, 'it was these two men here who did most of the work...'

'I'd say that's the least they could have done,' said the dead man, 'since they're the ones who buried me alive in the first place!' He shot them a disdainful glare. 'Absolute negligence! You're lucky I'm not a vindictive man, or I'd have both of you fired, and brought up on criminal charges!'

'Sorry, sir,' said one of the gravediggers. 'But everyone said you were dead. They even had a funeral. Your wife was here, weeping by your graveside just minutes ago!'

'Well, I'd say it's high time we set the record straight,

wouldn't you? Come on, take me to the town. I need to see the magistrate about this alleged death of mine! While I'm there, I'll arrange for my saviour here to get his just reward.'

'Yes sir,' said the gravediggers. 'Right away, sir!'

They ran off to retrieve a vehicle, leaving Narseh and the dead man in silence. The dead man shot Narseh a wink; Narseh winked back, then resumed his humble and innocent façade.

Soon the gravediggers returned in a mule-driven wagon. Narseh and the dead man climbed into the wagon bed and sat amidst the clinging smell of grave dirt. One of the diggers whipped the reins, driving the wagon through the cemetery gates and onto the dry earthen road which led to the town of Blackheart's Crossing. Parked by the highway were Narseh's own vehicles, a trio of luxurious coaches with black steeds in harnesses of bronze-studded leather. Slaves sat in the drivers' seats, waiting for their master's command. Narseh bid them to follow, and they lashed the reins, pursuing the wagon in a haze of rising dust.

It didn't take them long to reach the town. The place was a colony, built on conquered soil by the Republic of Kurolow. Like many such places it had been built to a formula, with a plaza in the centre surrounded by governmental buildings.

Narseh glanced at the towering structures dismissively. The town was not as shabby as others in this part of the world, but it could hardly compare with the grandeur of Alhazred, the place of his birth, where the towers of the Seven Sultans shone like jewels in the night, and plumes of rainbow fire danced through the deserts at dusk, smokeless and whirling on the sultry desert winds.

The vehicles stopped before the courthouse, and the dead man leapt from the wagon.

'Come on,' he said. 'Let's get this matter sorted. I don't much like being legally dead!'

Narseh and the gravediggers followed the dead man as he rushed into the courthouse past a pair of armed guards who looked quite surprised to see him. The guards followed after, and soon the whole group emerged into a large stone courtroom where a trio of magistrates were presiding over a trial. The trial was evidently not a grand matter; a scattering of spectators dotted the pews, and a solitary defendant stood with a hang-dog look in the desolate space before the judges' bench.

'Mister Amansovis,' said one of the magistrates. 'I hereby find you guilty of –'

The judge froze mid-sentence as the dead man rushed into the hall.

'Kruze?' said the judge with a look of surprise. 'Is that you?'

'It most certainly is!' snapped the dead man.

'But you're supposed to be dead!'

'I know. That's why I'm here!'

The gobsmacked magistrates glanced at one another, while the people in the pews began to whisper excitedly.

'Kruze is back!' they said.

'I thought he was dead?'

'We should've been so lucky!'

Kinevel Kruze had been a well-known member of the town, but not a well-liked one. His extravagant wealth had been equalled only by his hateful disposition. By his own stern request – and to the sorrow of none – the general public had been banned from attending his funeral. Presently he strode into the space before the judges, while Narseh and the gravediggers followed behind.

'I'm here to have my death certificate nullified!' snapped the dead man.

'Indeed,' said the judges. 'But we're rather in the middle of something...'

Kruze shot a glance at the defendant with the hang-dog look.

'In the middle of what?' he snapped. 'The piddling trial of some peasant cattle molester? By the dead gods below, I've come back from being buried alive!'

The judges glanced at one another, and nodded.

'Very well,' said the chief magistrate. 'In light of this incredible occurrence, I'm going to postpone the matter of the People Versus Amansovis, and open the court to this more important matter. Mister Kruze, please tell us the tale of your astonishing return from the grave.'

The bailiffs dragged away the distressed-looking Amansovis, while the dead man addressed the assembly.

'I will tell you my tale. But all I can tell you is that which I remember clearly. Yesterday – if indeed it really was yesterday, for the passage of time is somewhat muddy for me at the moment – I remember taking ill, and wanting to lie down. Then came a period of interminable blackness, as if some deep and mighty sleep had overcome me. The next thing I knew I was waking in darkness, surrounded by the stench of the grave, bounded by the timbers of a coffin sealed with nails. Filth sifted down upon my head through the splits in the timbers. I could hear the very worms crawling in the earth! I tried to break my way out of the casket, but the space was so confining I could barely move my arms. All I could do was bash my fists against the lid!'

He held up his hands, showing the scratches on his pale and puffy flesh. The audience, riveted, listened in amazement as the dead man continued.

'I screamed as loud as I could, for I fancied I could already feel the stagnant air beginning to run out. I'd begun to give up hope, when suddenly I heard a voice calling down through the earth, muffled by the dirt, but there all the same. It was the voice of that man there – that man, my saviour!'

The dead man whirled and pointed at Narseh.

'That man took note of my plight. That man dug the earth with his own noble hands. That man summoned these two moronic gravediggers from their bout of lazy drinking, and forced them to unearth me from the grave in which they had mistakenly laid me. If it wasn't for him, I'd be doomed. If it wasn't for him, I'd be worm-food. Saviour, please – tell me your name!'

'My name is Narseh Az-Pinah, from the land of Alhazred.'

The three judges glanced at one another, then turned to the witnesses.

'Is this true?' asked the chief magistrate.

'Yes, Your Honour,' said Narseh, affecting a humble demeanour.

'Yes, Your Honour,' said one of the gravediggers. 'Except that we weren't off drinking when it happened. We were starting to dig another grave...'

'A likely story,' hissed the dead man.

Ignoring both Kruze and the diggers, the judge turned to Narseh.

'It seems you're quite the hero, mister Az-Pinah. But tell me if you please, just what was a foreigner like you doing in a graveyard, here in Blackheart's Crossing?'

'Well,' said Narseh, 'recently I've been doing a bit of genealogical research, you see, during which time I discovered that a branch of my family hailed from this area. Being a man of some modest means, and dedicated above all to honouring the spirits of my poor departed kin, I undertook a mission to visit their places of rest, so I might supply them with gifts to enrich them in the afterlife. I was visiting just such a grave when I heard mister Kruze here struggling in his coffin...' Narseh put his hand on his heart, endeavouring to look as righteous as possible.

'Your familial piety is clearly to be commended, Mister Az-Pinah,' said the judge. 'But who, may I ask, was this long-lost relative of yours?'

Narseh paused, struggling to recall the ridiculous name from the grave he had randomly chosen. Panic rose within his breast as he suffered a bout of sudden mental blankness. Try as he might he couldn't recall the name, though it seemed to linger torturously on the edge of his thoughts. Seconds ticked by. He felt the scrutinizing gazes of all three judges fixed keenly upon him. A solitary droplet of sweat began to crawl down his forehead, and the room seemed somehow hotter. His entire precious scheme – perhaps even his liberty, his life – was now hanging by a thread of stubborn memory.

Fuck! he thought. *Curse your stupid name, Paerulicent Amberkance Perfleeticat the Third!*

With a sense of relief he composed himself, and repeated the name out loud for the judges to hear.

'You're sure he's a relative of yours?' asked one of the magistrates.

'Quite sure,' said Narseh. 'Although, to be fair, many of the records I've consulted are mouldering from age, as well as being filled with scribal errors. Still, I'd much rather pay my respects to a foreigner by accident, than miss out on honouring my very own kin through an excess of scholarly caution.'

'Well said,' said the dead man. 'Well said indeed. Truly you're a man of great character! Which is why I'd like to amend my will at once. Honoured judges, let the record state that Mister Narseh Az-Pinah of Alhazred is to receive half of my estate when I die!' A collective gasp rose up from the audience, while the dead man continued. 'And the other half is to be given to this fair town!'

A gasp of total shock rose up from the spectators. Could Kinevel Kruze, the notoriously miserly misanthrope, really be bequeathing his wealth to the people he'd treated with contempt for so long? The dead man strolled around, gesturing grandly.

'My brush with the grave has taught me a valuable lesson,' he said. 'When I was lying down there in the cold, sodden earth, feeling the dust of dead bodies defiling my lungs, I realized what a rotten human being I've been all these years. I want to make up for it. I want to give something back!'

'That's a very noble sentiment,' said the judge. 'But are you sure about all this? What about your wife?'

'Forget that stupid cow,' snapped the dead man. 'She's the one who buried me alive in the first place! I don't want to give her a crumb, the ungrateful bitch. No, my money shall go to Mister Az-Pinah, and to the town of Blackheart's Crossing.'

'I beg you to reconsider,' said Narseh. 'Surely your

poor wife should be forgiven –'

'No!' snapped the dead man. 'I'll hear no argument. My mind's made up!'

Narseh fell silent. The magistrates glanced at one another, and shrugged. They didn't want to argue too strongly – not when the dead man was trying to enrich their own coffers.

'Very well,' said the chief judge. 'Let the record show that Kinevel Kruze is alive, and that his estate upon his actual death shall be split equally between Mister Narseh Az-Pinah of Alhazred, and the town of Blackheart's Crossing.'

The scribe wrote the judgement in a ledger. No sooner had he done so than the dead man put a hand to his chest, let out a terrible groan, and fell to the floor with an echoing CRASH!

A bailiff rushed to check the dead man's breathing and pulse. With a look of alarm he turned to the judges. 'He's stone dead!'

Another gasp rose up from the audience.

'Poor man,' said Narseh. 'The strain of being buried alive must have killed him in the end.' He paused, glancing slyly at the magistrates. 'Still, I trust the court will honour his final request?'

***

Narseh grinned as his slaves loaded the last of Kruze's loot into the back of a carriage. Barely a week had gone by since Kinevel Kruze's second death, and already his estate had been liquidated, with half of the proceeds going to Narseh and the rest to the town's local government. Kinevel's widow had complained quite a lot in the interim, of course, but the judges hadn't listened.

Still smiling, Narseh climbed into the coach and strode between the stacked-up crates of gold, tapestries, and jewels. Beyond the crates was a door leading to a secret compartment, cunningly concealed amidst the cabin's baroque decor. After glancing around to make sure no one was watching, Narseh opened the door by use of a secret lever, then slipped inside, sealing the entrance behind him. There, sitting in the glimmer of a feeble lantern, was his girlfriend Wena.

Wena's emerald eyes stared up at him brightly. She hailed from the land of the necromancers, but had been banished by her brethren before being taught all of their magickal arts. Nevertheless she had managed to learn a few sorcerous tricks – including how to raise the dead into a semblance of life and take control of their bodies, just as she had done with Kinevel Kruze, who'd been dead as a doornail when they'd put him in the ground.

She rose up at once, embracing Narseh tightly. She was dressed in a cloak made from strips of black mummy wrap. The fabric had been soaked in putrescence and dried in the sun. Dried effluvium clung to the stiffened strips of linen, some of which bristled from her shoulders like the plumage of a vulture. Steeped in the energies of death, the garment served as a focus for her sorcery. It also stank horribly, though Narseh was more or less used to that by now.

What he wasn't quite used to was the stench of her body. She'd been cooped up in the coach for a week now, concealed from prying eyes, lest the people of Blackheart's Crossing should notice her presence and thereby uncover Narseh's trickery. Her only direct contact with other people during this time had been when Narseh's slaves had tended to her needs under cover of darkness, bringing her food and emptying her chamber pots. Greeted with her now, Narseh found her unwashed aroma, combined with the foetid bouquet of her cloak, almost unbearable. He recoiled from her embrace, and Wena stepped back, looking wounded.

'You've left me alone all this time,' she hissed, 'and now you won't even touch me?'

'I'm sorry, my dear,' he said. 'It's just that you're so very...stinky.'

'How do you think I feel?' she whispered. 'I've been stuck in this bloody compartment for days!'

'I know, my dear,' he said. 'And I'm so very sorry. It must have been awful for you, alone in this closet by yourself. It was a grim time for me, that's for sure, sleeping by my lonesome in that expensive hotel across the street. But it had to be done, for the sake of the job. Here, come to me...'

With a loving air he smiled and embraced her, braving the stench. For a moment she was sullen and limp in his arms. Then she squeezed him back tightly, and looked into his eyes.

'How did I do?' she asked.

'You were marvellous,' said Narseh. 'Your performance as Kinevel Kruze was amazing. Our job here is done, and we'll soon be away.'

She smiled and pulled him down for a kiss. Her breath was rank, but Narseh kissed her all the same. He had to keep her happy, after all – she was the key to his current success. And somewhere in his black soul was a spark of affection, like a crack in the facets of an ebony sapphire.

'What now?' she asked, when they finally broke off the kiss.

'First, I think we need to take you to a place where you can bathe, my dear,' he said, wrinkling his nose in an exaggerated manner.

Wena giggled in his arms.

'Then,' he said with a smile, 'then we'll be off some-place else, to find another dead man to fleece!'

Wena frowned. 'I'm not staying in the coach this time, Narseh.'

'That's okay, my dove. We'll find a way to have you stay with me this time, I promise.'

Her frown began to soften, but only a little. 'Are you sure we should do this again, quite so soon?'

'Indeed, my dear. This scam worked a treat! We only made one minor mistake.'

'What's that?'

'We shouldn't have given any money to the state. We should've seized it all!'

'But giving that money to the council got them play-ing on our side!'

'I know,' he said. 'Believe me, I know. You should

have seen the greed flashing through the eyes of those judges…!'

It was almost like looking in a mirror, he thought. Then he added: 'Still, it's not really fair they should reap the rewards of our labour, now is it? After all, we're the ones bringing back the bodies. They're just sitting on their arses.'

'But if the magistrates don't support our case, then we'll end up with nothing! What if the dead man's heirs should contest the new will? What if we have to go through a trial? The longer we get stuck in some town, fighting in court, the greater the chance they'll uncover the trick!'

'You worry too much, my sweet,' he said, stroking her cheek. 'This scheme is foolproof. Nothing can go wrong!'

Wena smiled back and stayed silent, even while the sound of alarm bells clanged in her head.

Chapter 3: The Hashishan

The hashishan flitted like a shadow through the tunnels of the derelict sewer system. The place was as dry and as dusty as a tomb. Very few people even knew of its existence, though it ran beneath the streets of the town like veins beneath the skin of a cadaver.

Moving by the light of a solitary taper, the hashishan spied his destination up ahead: a timber ladder ascending to a trapdoor. The bricks around the trapdoor, though pitted and old, were not yet as weathered as those which surrounded them, suggesting the door had been built many decades or centuries after the sewer itself had first been completed.

The hashishan stopped a few feet short of the ladder. He placed the taper in his teeth and removed a pipe from his pocket. The pipe was a luxurious piece, its ebony surface engraved with cavorting demons whose bodies seemed to be congealing from stylized billows of smoke. The most conspicuous figure of all was that of

Soaefoth, the demon sloth himself, in whose perenni-
ally stoned and sleepy eyes lurked glimmers of eldritch
might and ancient deicide.

The hashishan gazed at the familiar image for a moment, then placed the pipe between his thighs as he removed from his cloak a small leather pouch from which
issued a moist and minty aroma. The smell grew stronger as he opened the pouch to reveal a quarter-ounce of
black and resinous weed. He sniffed the weed with delight, then stuffed a single bud into the pipe before re-
turning the pouch to his pocket. Taking the taper from
betwixt his teeth and placing the pipe to his lips, he
fired up the bud and began to inhale. The taper's flame
dove into the bowl, plunging the tunnel into almost
total darkness. The bud's outer surface flickered and
flared like the skin of a meteor skimming the heavens.
Smoke tendrils stretched through the filter and into
the hashishan's well-trained lungs, where they coiled
and sat, soaking deep into the scarred airways, till at
last their dregs were exhaled in a roiling plume which

looked almost solid in the shadows of the sewer.

Sweet euphoria cradled the hashishan's head. The black weed was strong. It might have made another man sleepy or lazy, but the hashishan had been trained to use the narcotic differently. Focusing his mind through the haze, he entered a self-induced trance.

Much of his psyche grew dormant. His jabbering thoughts, his preoccupations, his fears, even his present anxiety as he stood on the cusp of his murderous mission – all these things and more melted away into the dark recesses of his consciousness, until all he felt was an uncanny sense of his immediate surroundings.

The dry air of the sewer felt suddenly cooler and more tangible. He could feel its subtle caress on his skin with immaculate precision, as if each and every hair on his body were a separate sensory organ attuned to the atmosphere around him. He seemed to depart from the prosaic flow of ordinary space and time, becoming a stranger to himself, a stranger in a new, weird world where anything could happen, and where he could do anything – he could steal, he could sneak, he could murder, all with a smooth and disassociated ease.

Replacing the pipe in his pocket and the taper back betwixt his teeth he began to ascend the wooden ladder. Gingerly he did so, for the frame and the rungs were old and rotting. They creaked with protest even from the burden of his slender weight.

Soon he reached the trapdoor and carefully began to push it upwards. The metal felt scabrous with rust. The hinges creaked softly. Flakes of iron fell upon his face. Holding the trapdoor upraised, he slipped through the crack before closing the portal softly behind him.

The hashishan had emerged into a cramped, dusty corridor. Looking down, he saw the remains of the chain and padlock that had once secured the trapdoor, lying rusted and broken with age. They seemed to have lain undisturbed for a very long time. So far, everything his employers had told him was accurate. Thanks to them, he knew he was now above ground, in a secret passage concealed within the villa of the man he'd come to murder.

Onwards he crept down the corridor. Soon he arrived at a door on the left. Feeling calm but alert he snuffed out the taper, opened the door, and stepped into silvery shadows. He'd emerged exactly where his employers had told him he would – in the old miser's trophy room. Moonbeams filtered through a series of iron-barred windows, shedding their gleam on the pelts and severed heads which adorned the room. Here was a lion's pelt splayed on the ground; there was a rhino's head mounted on a wall, its horn adorned with intricate carvings; here was the body of a neonate white wyrm, its lamprey-like mouth fixed into a permanent gape by the taxidermist's art. All the pieces were immaculately clean, for the miser was not miserly at all when it came to the upkeep of his trophies and relics.

The hashishan crept from the room into the network of hallways beyond. The villa was opulent and massive, but mostly unpeopled, save for the miser and his small staff of servants, most of whom were presently sleeping. The miser had guards, but only a few of them. They talked loudly as they made their rounds, and their footfalls echoed ahead of them, allowing the hashishan to easily avoid them. Onwards he crept through the corridors, bypassing rooms filled with the harvest of avarice. There were luxurious bathrooms with large marble pools, chambers with silver and gold statues on display, and beautiful atriums inlaid with mosaics of jewels and precious stones.

Soon he arrived outside the old miser's study. The door was ajar, and the light of a fitful lantern spilled into the hallway, ruffling the shadows on the walls. The old man was up late pouring over his papers, just as the hashishan's employers had predicted.

The hashishan drew closer to the door. Now that he was so close to his goal, he could feel a sense of excitement and dread begin to bubble up from the depths of his mind, threatening to taint the perfection of his trance. He paused, focused his mind, and banished all emotion. Once again he felt nothing but crystalline awareness, mixed with his murderous imperative.

He peered through the doorway into the study. Seated at a desk inside was the miser himself, perusing his ledgers and books. The man's name was Muragar Zak. He was hoary but healthy in his age. An old man like that might live to be a hundred years old, hence why his embittered descendants had hired the hashishan. But Muragar's death had to look natural, or at least like an accident, otherwise suspicion might be cast upon them. Luckily the hashishan had means of making the death look prosaic. In his pocket, next to his pipe and his bag of weed, was a vial of potent venom milked from the fangs of a Thunian singing snake. A single droplet introduced into the bloodstream was enough to bring about an almost instant cardiac arrest.

The hashishan took out the vial, carefully unstoppered the cap, and dipped a small needle into the acrid-smelling liquid within. His weapon was ready; now all he had to do was administer the sting. But how to get close? He couldn't cross the room without exposing himself to the risk of being seen. If the old man caught a glimpse of him – even for a moment – he might just have enough time to sound the alarm before the hashishan closed the distance. And even if the old man was unable to summon his guards, he could still try to fight back against the intruder. The hashishan was confident he could easily triumph in any such conflict, but that wasn't the problem. Any scuffle, no matter how brief or one-sided, could result in tell-tale bruises or marks being left on the old miser's body, making the death look suspicious. No, he had to get close by some other means. There was nothing else for it – he'd have to use the Demon Arts of Death.

He focused his mind, picturing the demonic runes his master had taught him. Some practitioners of the Demon Arts – like the knights of the Order of Chaos – carved the runes on their weapons, and made use of them that way. The hashishan often laughed when he thought about such amateurs. For his master had taught him to internalize the power of the runes completely.

Now they were so much a part of the hashishan that they seemed to be branded on his soul, or enshrined in the palace of his mind, like frescoes in cerebral halls.

He pictured the full sequence of runes he needed, then stepped into a thick patch of darkness on the wall. The darkness gave way like cool air. He found himself walking in a murky netherworld, surrounded by infinite shadows. The air was almost unbearably cold. The overlapping shadows contorted, taking on the likeness of stupefying tapestries, each covered with an intricate pattern. The hashishan experienced a moment of terrible vertigo. It felt as if each fleeting, shadowy pattern were tugging at him, trying to pull him toward it. Each pattern, he knew, was a door to a corresponding pocket of darkness which existed somewhere in the universe. Many were the doors which might lead to a place of certain doom, or to some distant corner of the fathomless cosmos, where a person could wander till death, lost and alone. In truth, there was only one path he wanted, one path he'd trained his bloodshot eyes on since traversing the breach into the shadowverse. He followed that path –

And crawled out into the shadows beneath the miser's desk. His body trembled from the residual coldness of the realm he had traversed, and tiny icicles clung to his clothing. Too much longer in the shadowverse and he would have risked death from exposure. Only powerful beings like cosmic demons could travel those highways of darkness for any length of time, for their bodies were immune to the cold and their minds were resistant to the maddening patterns of the myriad shadow gates. As for the hashishan, he was only a mortal. He hunched into a ball, reeling from the shock of his journey. He clenched his jaw to stop his teeth from chattering, and fought to control his quaking limbs. The miser's legs were just inches away, close enough to make the kill – and yet his quivering hand could barely keep a hold on the poison-tipped needle.

The miser stirred in his chair, as if somehow aware that something was wrong. There was no more time for the hashishan to marshal his strength. With trembling hand the stabbed the needle towards the old man's naked foot. It struck between the toes. The miser's voice rose up in a cry –

But only for a moment. The rising sound died. The miser convulsed in his chair. The hashishan slipped out from under the desk and stood beside his victim. The old man was clutching at his heart with a white-knuckled hand. His eyes rolled back to the whites. He seized, then shook, then slumped onto the desk. Rivulets of ink spilled across his ledgers as his falling body overturned the inkpot.

The hashishan craned his ear. The villa was silent. He embedded the needle's poisoned tip into a cork, wrapped both up in leather, and carefully placed the resulting parcel into his pocket, planning to dispose of it later. He watched the miser's chest for movement, but it was utterly still. He took a small mirror from his pocket and held it to the miser's mouth, looking for any sign of breath escaping the lips. There was none. He checked the old man's radial artery for a pulse. There was none. He checked the carotid, and found nothing there either.

The miser was dead. Emerging partway from his narcotic trance, the hashishan permitted himself a satisfied smile. His work here was done. The old man had died of a heart attack, and no one would notice the venom in his veins, nor the tiny pinprick on his foot.

All that remained for the hashishan was the relatively simple task of escaping the villa without being seen. Then he'd simply have to lie low and wait until it was time to take payment for his services. Usually, he only took a job if at least half of the money was provided upfront. But this job was different. The miser's heirs, united in their murderous conspiracy, had offered the hashishan five times his normal fee. The only catch was that they couldn't afford to pay him until the old man's estate had been divided among them, for such was the miser's stinginess that all of them were presently living in poverty. The hashishan had accepted the arrangement without much complaint. For the amount being offered, he was happy to postpone his payday, at least for a little while. And should his employers – or anyone else – try to get between him and his fee, he'd simply kill them all, and take what was owed from their lifeless bodies.

Chapter 4: At Midday I Will Possess Your Corpse

'It's perfect!' said Narseh as he knelt before Wena in the coach's secret compartment. 'There's a funeral going on right now. I heard about it earlier, when I was taking my lunch in the town. The man was a rich old miser. He had himself a gigantic villa, all filled up with riches he'd been hoarding for years. His descendants haven't even got a crumb!' He paused, smiling mischievously. 'I bet they're excited. I bet they're looking forward to a great big payday. Well, sucks to be them – because we're gonna swoop in and take the whole lot!'

'Are you sure?' asked the necromancer. 'I mean, maybe we should only take half. Or two-thirds. They'll be a lot less likely to put up a fight, if we leave them with something...'

'Nonsense, my sweet. It's all or nothing!'

'But surely they'll fight it in court...'

'Let them fight,' he said. 'It won't do them any good. We'll make this one foolproof. This time I want you to make that corpse look as truly alive as you possibly can. Make his heart beat in his chest and his veins throb with blood. Convince them the dead man is of sound mind and body, and acting of his own free will. Then, and only then, will our benefactor "die" once again. Can you do that?'

'Yes,' she said. 'But – '

'No buts,' he said, pressing her lips shut with his finger. 'We're not at home to Mister Negative, my sweet. Besides, I have absolute confidence in you.' He smiled and gazed into her eyes, until Wena felt confident too. 'And now I must away to buy some flowers, and take up my position in the cemetery. Wait for the signal, then do as before.'

He rose, then stooped to give her a parting kiss on the mouth. Wena wrapped her arms around his shoulders, holding him close and kissing him fervently back. She reluctantly let go as she felt him pull away.

'Don't worry about a thing, my dear,' he said. 'I believe in you. We're going to get all of that money. And when we're done, we'll take a break for a while and just be together, you and me.'

'You promise?'

'I promise,' he said.

They shared a warm smile, and Narseh slipped from the compartment, pulling the door closed behind him. Wena sat alone in the light of a feeble red lantern, waiting. For a time the smile remained on her lips. His presence and his words had melted her misgivings, filling her with confidence. But now that he was gone, doubts began to creep into her mind once again, doubts that had plagued her on and off since the two had first met.

Was Narseh just using her, stringing her along for the sake of her necromantic arts? Did he even really love her at all? He told her he did, but she couldn't be sure. Perhaps all he really loved was money, and the process of acquiring it. He kept dragging her into these criminal schemes. Often she tried to protest, but somehow he always knew just what to say to get her back onboard. Sometimes she felt as though she were trapped in his orbit, like the moon around the earth, bound by the power of his words and the gravity of his will.

Perhaps she was weak. Perhaps she was merely in love. His smile made her melt; his caresses got her wet. And she couldn't deny that their crimes were often exciting, not to mention rewarding. And yet, there was a part of her psyche that screamed out in protest. A part that disliked being trapped in his orbit. A part of her, perhaps, that even resented her lover. It was silent when Narseh was near, as if smothered or negated by the pleasure of his company. But when he was gone – as he was at that moment – she felt that rebelliousness well up inside her, like the pangs of a stomach ache.

Maybe our relationship is poisoned? she wondered, and not for the first time.

Then she thought of his words, about his pledge that they would both take a break once this job was completed. She hoped it was true. She longed for a brief respite from all this scheming, scamming, and stealing. An oasis of pleasure in a desert of greed, where there would only be love and its joyful expression.

A knock on the door of the compartment jarred her from her thoughts. Narseh's slaves had been watching the cemetery gates, waiting for the funeral to finish and the mourners to depart. Their knocking was her cue to take possession of the corpse!

Wena closed her eyes and began to meditate. With practiced ease her psyche slipped loose from her physical body and hovered invisibly above it. Some sorcerers could travel almost anywhere like that – across the starry void, between dimensional membranes, even through the stubborn mists of time. But being the soul of a necromancer, Wena's astral spirit could only travel like a magnet drawn toward the energies of death.

Wena's astral form flew from the coach toward the cemetery. Like a ghost she passed through the bodies of mourners emerging from the gates. Some of them flinched or recoiled, as if a chill wind had suddenly caressed them. Wena sensed them from the inside as her astral form briefly occupied the same space as their internal organs. Their insides were opaque to her sight, but she could feel their beating hearts, their breathing lungs, the warmth of the blood as it pulsed through arteries and veins. Her essence fled from such things, conditioned as it was to seek the miasma of the dead.

Wena's essence flew through the graveyard like a bird of prey. Each time she flew above a grave she felt herself drawn towards the worm-eaten flesh of the body below. Her astral form, long tainted by the art of necromancy, instinctively longed to anchor itself in the flesh and bones of the dead.

Resisting the pull of each cadaver, Wena flew on towards her true target. Soon she saw Narseh ahead, kneeling before a grave with a bouquet of flowers in hand. She passed through his flesh, briefly wondering if she could somehow sense the spark of his love for her somewhere within him. All she felt was the pulse of his blood, quickened by the thrill of the score that awaited.

A dozen feet from Narseh lay the miser's fresh grave. Wena flew down into the soil and felt the strong pull of the corpse, which due to its freshness was teeming with necromantic energy.

Wena let her soul sink into the corpse and settle into place. She felt the dead flesh around her psyche like a suit. It teemed with newborn rot. The miser's corpse had only just begun to break down. In a few more days it would be bloated with gases, parts of it swollen like pieces of nightmare fruit. The stench would be appalling. For now, however, it could still be mistaken for the body of a living man – especially with a little help from Wena's magick.

She quickly went to work arresting the process of decay. Perhaps if she had studied harder during her abortive stint at necromancy school she would have discovered the traces of venom still lingering in the corpse's veins, and would have known the old miser was a victim of foul play. Instead she noticed nothing untoward, and simply completed her spell, stalling the process of decomposition and imbuing the corpse with an illusory semblance of life.

'Help!' she shouted in the voice of the dead man, as she hammered with his fists against the lid of the coffin.

Chapter 5: Return of the Miser

'Woo-hoo!' shouted Ninia Zak, granddaughter of Muragar Zak. 'The old bastard's dead!'

She raised her goblet in a toast. The rest of the heirs toasted back. There was Ninia's younger brother, Gerebrah Zak; her even younger brother, Dalmion Zak; her younger sister, Soronia Zak; and her two cousins, Yellen Zak and Merekin Zak. Together they represented all the living adult members of the Zak family. They also represented the members of a criminal conspiracy responsible for Muragar's assassination at the hands of the hashishan. Ninia was the ringleader. It was she who had convinced the other five to go along with the plan. She was thirty years old, and tired of being poor. Why should the whole family languish in poverty while Muragar sat fat atop a giant heap of silver and gold? Ninia's children deserved better. They all deserved better.

It hadn't taken much work to get the others to go along with her plan. And so here they were, shouting with joy and clinking their goblets. Not that the goblets made an actual clinking sound. The vessels were cheap timber cups which sometimes left splinters in Ninia's mouth. It was true – she and her co-conspirators couldn't even afford decent tableware!

But soon that would all change. Now that the old man was dead, it was only a matter of time until his estate was divided amongst them. Then they would drink from vessels of gold in the old miser's villa, in which they would dwell like a true family, and that vast edifice, which for so long had been a realm of silent avarice, would transform into a place of laughter and life. It was a dream come true! And Ninia had made it come true, through her very own boldness and firm resolution.

She couldn't be happier. She smiled at her family, and they smiled back.

The moment was shattered by a rapping at the door. Ninia's younger brother Gerebrah opened it, revealing a neighbour who stood panting on the steps as though he'd been jogging. His eyes were wide with amazement.

'You won't believe it,' he said. 'Your grandfather's alive. Someone dug him up from the grave. He's over in the courthouse right now!'

Silence fell over the room as the conspirators traded looks of shock and apprehension.

'Is this some sick joke?' asked Ninia. 'Because it isn't very funny!'

'I'm not joking!' said the neighbour. 'Come see for yourself if you don't believe me!'

The Zaks traded wary glances, then headed off at once to the courthouse, leaving their children at home. It took them a while to arrive, for their ramshackle houses were located in a poor part of town far from the majestic buildings of state. When they finally rushed through the doors of the courthouse, all of them froze in amazement. There, before the judges, was the rotten old miser himself, in the process of addressing the court. Standing beside him was a stranger with a turban and a crescent-shaped beard. Judging by his clothes, Ninia guessed the stranger must have hailed from Alhazred, the land of smokeless fire. And yet, Ninia had greater things to worry about than this man's provenance. Her grandfather seemed to be alive! Could it be the hashis-han had fouled up the job? No, that seemed impossible. Ninia had seen Muragar's body for herself. She'd even checked his pulse. He'd been dead as a doornail! Bewildered, she watched the dead man raise his hand and continue to address the court.

'And so I,' said the dead man, 'Muragar Zak, being of sound mind and body, and under no compulsion whatsoever, hereby bequeath all my worldly positions, at the time of my death, to my noble friend and saviour, Mister Narseh Az-Pinah.'

The spectators whispered in amazement.

'What the FUCK!' shouted Ninia, unable to control herself.

The dead man glanced at her, then turned to the judges.

'Your Honour, can you please tell this woman to be quiet?'

The judges peered back at him with worried expressions.

'Mister Zak,' said one of them, 'surely you recognise your very own granddaughter?'

Oh shit, thought Wena as she peered through the dead man's eyes at the group of shocked strangers in the doorway. *The guy's family's here – and I don't know their names, or anything about them! If I'm not careful, I could ruin it all.*

She glanced at Narseh, catching a glimmer of concern in his eyes. She knew she had to fix this – fast.

'I see no family before me!' yelled Wena in a voice not her own. 'This bunch of ingrates are the ones who sought to bury me alive. From now on I shan't speak their names, nor even look at them at all if I can help it. They're dead to me, the lot of them!'

Murmurs of surprise spread through the courtroom, while Narseh tried to hide a creeping smile.

'And now,' said the dead man, 'I'd like to get this matter over with conclusively. I invite any physician in attendance to check both my physical and mental health at once. I want there to be no doubt whatsoever in the eyes of the court that my state of mind is perfectly sound, and that my brush with death has only made me stronger in will.'

The judges nodded. Soon a physician arrived and escorted the dead man to an antechamber. Ninia Zak waited in agonized suspense. Her mind whirled with confusion. How was this possible? She'd seen the miser's corpse just yesterday. And yet here he was, right before her eyes, talking, walking, and breathing.

Is it some kind of sorcery? she wondered. *Or is the old man just too mean to die? Maybe something went wrong with the assassin's poison. Maybe it just made him look dead for a while!*

Dozens of possible scenarios flitted through Ninia's mind. And yet, what occupied her thoughts most of all was the prospect of losing all that money. She could almost feel all that cash slipping through her fingers like ephemeral sand. Fervently she hoped the old man would somehow fail the physician's exam.

Let him be pronounced a lunatic, she thought. *Let the whole thing be revealed as a sorcerer's scam! For surely no sorcerer could fool a learned physician...*

While Ninia fretted, Wena sat in the antechamber, dressed in the flesh of the dead man, undergoing a battery of tests. First the physician asked her a series of general knowledge questions, such as what year it was, who the reigning archon was, what important events had occurred in the region, and so on. Wena passed the test with flying colours. She was glad he hadn't asked more specific or localized questions, or indeed any questions about the dead man himself, about whom she knew very little. Then he showed her pictures of animals and objects, asking her to name them. She aced that test too. So far, it was child's play.

After that came the physical exam, which was far more difficult. Wena had to pump stagnant blood through the dead man's vessels to simulate a heartbeat. She had to suck breath into his stiffened airways, then pump it back out to simulate his breathing. She had to warm his cold flesh, moisten his dry lips, banish the burgeoning stench of decay. The effort was draining – but in the end, it paid off.

'Muragar Zak is of sound mind and body,' said the physician as they returned to the courtroom.

Ninia Zak felt her heart sink.

'In that case,' said the senior judge, 'I have no choice but to endorse Zak's new living testament. Let the record bear witness!'

The courtroom scribe entered the decree. No sooner had he done so than Muragar Zak grasped his chest, screamed, and hit the floor with a CRASH!

The physician sped to the body, checking it for signs of life. A few moments later he looked up and shook his head.

'He's dead, Your Honour,' he said.

The spectators gasped. So did Ninia.

'Such a tragedy,' said Narseh. 'The stress of being buried alive must have killed him in the end. Still, I trust the court will honour his request. Seeing as how he was of sound mind and body...'

'No way!' shouted Ninia, rushing to the front of the court with the rest of her relatives. 'We're the family. It's only fair that we inherit! We'd like to contest the will.'

I knew this would happen, thought Wena as she lay on the floor, still cloaked in the dead man's flesh, peering through his fixed eyes.

Narseh turned to Ninia. 'My heart grieves for your loss, Mrs...'

'Ninia Zak,' she said.

'Mrs. Ninia Zak. Such a tragedy that you should lose your dear grandfather twice in one week. And, to be honest, I find his final testament somewhat unseemly. To deny one's own family their rightful inheritance, even for the heinous act of burying one's body alive, seems overly punitive to my mind. Certainly I, given the choice, would never even dream to deny you your birthright. Indeed, for me, this unexpected offer of wealth feels much like a burden...'

'Then hand it over!' she said.

Narseh shook his head with an appearance of sadness. 'Would that I could. And yet, I fear that I must honour this man's most solemn request, regardless of my own feelings, lest I might anger his spirit in the underworld…'

I can't believe this shit! thought Ninia, glaring at Narseh. *Who is this bastard?!*

She turned to glare at the judges.

'You can't possibly do this,' she said. 'Even if grandfather was in his right mind – and I'm not really sure that he was – still, this request – this request is appalling! To give all that money to a stranger, to a foreigner, it's – it's unthinkable! It's against all the laws of tradition!'

'And yet that is what he asked for,' said Narseh. 'And who are we to defile a man's last living wishes on this earth?'

The judges motioned for silence, then whispered to each other. At length they turned back to the parties before them.

'Whilst it is true that Muragar Zak made this request of his own free will, it is indeed very irregular, and goes against precedent. Because of this, we would like to schedule a full and proper hearing, to take place next week. In the meantime, Muragar Zak's possessions will be held in trust by the state, until such time as this matter be resolved.'

Fuck, thought Narseh.

Yes! thought Ninia.

Narseh cleared his throat. 'A sage judgement, Your Honours,' he said. 'Your wisdom is truly commendable, and I shall abide by your ultimate decision, whatever it may be. And yet, there is one concession I might ask for...'

'Yes?' asked a judge.

'Well,' he said, 'it's just that I'm a man of modest means, you see.' Narseh held his hands together like a humble orphan begging for food. 'As you know, I'm currently on a sojourn to visit the graves of my many long-lost relatives. This endeavour, though dear to my heart, has unfortunately used up almost all of my wealth, so that all I have at present are the clothes on my back, some sundry possessions, a few dozen slaves, and the trio of coaches parked outside. Thusly I fear I can't afford to pay for any lodgings. If I'm to stay in this town throughout the course of this trial, I'd be forced to sleep in the back of a carriage, in stifling and humid confinement, which, as I'm sure you'll agree, is scarcely a fit place for any human being to reside in, and would certainly prove to be an unfair disadvantage when it came time for me to take part in the proceedings of this honourable court. And, since I'm assuming my opponents in this case all have their own stable lodgings…'

'What're you getting at, Mister Narseh?'

'Well,' he said. 'Might I be able to stay in the dead man's villa?'

Ninia gritted her teeth at the thought of this unctuous stranger staying in the home her family had built. It felt like desecration! Then she remembered the secret entrance she and her brothers had discovered while playing there as children. The same secret entrance the hashishan had so recently used – and which he could easily use again, should the need arise. A sinister smile flashed across her face, ever so briefly.

'The Zak family is happy for the stranger to stay at our villa,' she said.

The three judges, who had not yet finished their deliberations, shrugged at one another and granted her seemingly gracious request.

'Very well,' said one of them. 'Mister Az-Pinah will have use of the villa throughout the course of the trial until a final verdict is reached. But none of the objects therein may be disturbed. Is that clear?'

'I wouldn't dream of it,' said Narseh with his hand over his heart.

'Then this matter is adjourned for the moment. We shall proceed on the Ides of Iscariot!'

A few moments later, Ninia emerged from the courthouse with the rest of the Zaks. They watched as the man from Alhazred climbed into a fancy-looking coach and drove off towards the villa.

'What now, sis?' asked Gerebrah Zak.

'Now?' said Ninia. 'Now he have a talk with the hashishan!'

Chapter 6: Plans like Smoke

The hashishan sat on a rickety chair in Ninia's kitchen. Ninia and the rest of the conspirators were gathered around him in the cramped and dismal room. The hearth shed fitful light on their faces. They all looked anxious – save the hashishan, whose expression was tranquil. The smoke from his pipe hung thick in the air, for the windows and doors had all been sealed lest some neighbour should spy on the conspiracy. The smoke was potent; Ninia could already feel the beginnings of a second-hand high. She coughed into the crook of her arm, and wondered how the assassin could function with such a powerful narcotic in his system. Every time she'd seen him, he'd been smoking his pipe.

The guy must be high all day long, she thought. *He's probably got an incredible tolerance.*

So far he hadn't said much at all, and neither had they. Presently he peered at the Zaks, noting their anxious expressions. His bloodshot eyes were a startling blue.

'Is there a problem?' he asked.

'You bet there's a problem,' said Ninia. 'The man we hired you to kill wasn't dead!'

She launched into a hurried explanation of the afternoon's events – how her grandfather had apparently awoken in the grave, only to be rescued by a stranger from Alhazred, to whom he then bequeathed all his wealth, just before dropping dead in the middle of the courthouse.

'Most peculiar,' said the hashishan.

'No shit it's peculiar!' said Ninia.

'Still,' he said, after exhaling more smoke, 'there's no way your grandfather was alive.'

'But we saw it with our own eyes!' said Gerebrah Zak. 'Plus, I've heard of things happening like this before. People seem dead, but they're only asleep. Then later they wake up, sometimes even after they've been buried…'

'Impossible,' said the hashishan. 'Muragar was dead

when I left him. And trust me, boy, I know. Death is my business.'

'Then how do you explain it?' asked Ninia.

'The only explanation is sorcery. As far as I know, there are only two types of beings capable of raising the dead like that. The first are cosmic demons. The second are the necromancers of Khem.'

'But this guy's not from Khem,' said Ninia. 'He's from Alhazred.'

'Then he must have an accomplice, or a patron, working in the shadows.'

'So you're saying he's a thief?' said Gerebrah. 'That this is all some kind of magickal scam?'

The hashishan nodded.

'Well then we have to expose them. Right?' said Gerebrah, glancing around.

Ninia shook her head. 'We're not going to expose them,' she said. 'We're going to kill them. These bastards have to pay for what they've done!' She turned to the assassin. 'They're staying in the villa right now. I want you to sneak back in there and slaughter them all, then make their bodies and their coaches disappear, along with some of grandfather's wealth. The judges will conclude that they were thieves who've fled in the night. Then grandfather's estate will be transferred back to us, and we can pay you what we owe.'

The hashishan took a long drag from his pipe as he considered her proposal.

'That's a lot of slaughter,' he said. 'It's going to cost you a lot – quadruple what you already owe.'

Ninia winced. That was a lot of money. And yet, it was nothing compared with the vastness of Muragar's fortune.

'You've got a deal,' she said, extending her hand.

The hashishan shook it, and smiled.

***

Narseh strode through the villa, peering at the wealth on display. Racks of embossed silver plate; trunks of gold and jewels; statues of marble, carnelian, and jade – the riches seemed endless. A pair of his most educated slaves followed him with ledgers, taking a detailed inventory of the villa's many treasures, along with their approximate value. So far the overall figure was very, very high.

Narseh turned to Wena, who'd been smuggled from the coach to the villa in the folds of a carpet.

'We've hit the jackpot, my sweet!' he said with a smile.

'Are you sure we should be celebrating yet?' she asked. 'There's still the court case to consider...'

'Bah!' said Narseh. 'There's no way the court will overturn the will completely. The best those wretched relatives can hope for is a percentage – half, at the most. And long before that can even happen, we'll gather up the best of the treasures and bury them outside the town, so we can dig them up later. Face it, my dear – no matter what happens, we'll be making a killing!'

He smiled at her again, and Wena smiled back, though her worries remained.

'But aren't you concerned at all?' she said. 'And don't you think it's odd that they agreed to us staying here so quickly? What if they're planning something rotten?'

Narseh scoffed again. 'You worry too much, my dear. Besides, even if they are planning something, what can they do? I've got slaves standing guard at every entrance. And you've got sentries of your own to watch over us – and your guards don't sleep.'

He gestured to the pair of undead servants who followed in the necromancer's wake. Their bodies had been dried in natron and wrapped in emerald linen which matched the hue of Wena's eyes. Their own eyes had been scooped out and replaced with polished onyx. Their organs had likewise been removed, replaced with a mixture of sawdust and dried roses, which covered their musty odour with a sweeter perfume. Each zombie wore a cloak, and carried a khopesh. Their presence was indeed a comfort to Wena, for they would never tire, never sleep, never shirk from duty so long as she lived, and they themselves could only be destroyed through total dismemberment. They were in many ways the perfect guardians. And yet, she still felt worried.

Narseh caught the look in her eyes and clasped her hands in his.

'Stop fretting, my sweet,' he said. 'Come on – let me show you the master bedroom!'

He led her through the halls. The zombies followed after, while the slaves stayed behind to continue the stocktake.

Soon they arrived at a sumptuous chamber. The marble walls were adorned with silken brocade which shimmered in the light of a crystal chandelier. In the centre of the room was a four-poster bed with velvet curtains and piles of plump cushions on a fat feather mattress. And yet the most breathtaking sight of all was the huge pile of treasure piled around the bed – stacks of polished gold, heaps of silver plate, and mounds of gemstones which gleamed in a dozen different colours.

'Beautiful, isn't it?' said Narseh. 'I had the slaves bring it here earlier. Of course it will all have to be taken out soon, and buried for safekeeping. Still, I thought it might be nice to recline amidst the fruits of our labours. Don't you?'

Wena glanced around, feeling a pulse of excitement at the sight of all that treasure. Perhaps Narseh's greed was infecting her? And yet, more than she wanted the gold she wanted him. She wanted his passion, however grudging and rare it seemed to be.

She kissed him on the lips. This time he did not recoil, as he had in the coach – for this time her body was washed and her stinking cloak was on a hangar by the villa's front door.

Soon they were lying on the silken bedsheets. Wena was naked save for her black wig. Narseh was completely naked. He'd even taken off his turban, allowing his dark locks to cascade down his shoulders and over his chest.

Wena eyed him hungrily. He might have been greedy, but he wasn't a glutton. His body was lean from his restless lifestyle. He lay on his back with his prick standing up. She grasped it, feeling the pulse of warm blood beneath the skin. His hand found her cunt and fingered her throbbing clit. Both of them were ready.

She straddled his lap, and was about to mount him face-to-face, when he took her by the waist and began gently turning her away.

'Face the other way, please,' he said. 'I want to see your peachy rump...'

Wena paused. She liked being able to look him in the eyes when they made love. But she also liked pleasing him, and he seemed so keen to get a look at her butt. She turned around to face the shuttered door, then guided him inside her, humming with delight as she felt him within. The exquisite shock of entry was a novelty that never grew old. Moaning she rode him, slowly at first, then faster and faster, feeling the pleasure build higher and higher.

Meanwhile Narseh lay with his head on the pillows, watching her move. She was slender and dark. Her butt was firm and taut, like a ripening peach. He gripped it with his hands and ran his fingers up her waist, caught up in the luxury of looking at her. She was so very beautiful. And yet...

And yet there was all of that treasure nearby. His gaze moved past her, taking in the sight of silver and gold. Lying on the bed, he couldn't see the floor, just piles of gleaming riches sprawling out toward the walls.

He imagined the bed was adrift on an ocean of wealth. He imagined the rocking of the bed was the gentle susurration of those gleaming, golden waves. He focused his eyes back on Wena; he focused his eyes back on the gold; then he unfocused them completely, so that Wena was a black silhouette backed by an ocean of riches. It seemed to be the best of both worlds, and he moaned with delight.

Wena moaned too. Her movements grew erratic as the climax shook her body. Narseh surrendered and exploded inside her. As the orgasm gripping him, his vision grew even more blurred, and for a moment Wena vanished from his gaze, her dark silhouette eclipsed by the gleam of the gold.

Afterwards they lay on the bed, drinking wine and eating sweets. Wena smiled at Narseh, flushed in the afterglow. Her worries were gone for the moment, silenced by an onslaught of pleasure. Just for a second, she felt like there was nothing that could possibly go wrong.

***

The hashishan lurked in the shadows of the trophy room, watching the doorway. He'd gained access to the villa using the same secret entrance as last time. But from here on it seemed this mission would be harder than the last one. The hallways were crawling with armed guards. Judging from their clothing they were slaves from Alhazred. Chattel, but deadly nonetheless. The hashishan had watched them for a while now, building up a picture of their movements and trying to estimate their numbers. They patrolled in pairs, strolling the corridors with irritating frequency. Presently two of them were passing through the hallway outside.

The hashishan reached for his blade – then stopped. Cutting them down would be easy enough, but these people were supposed to disappear into the night; there couldn't be bloodstains, not if he could help it. So what then? He could sneak up behind them, break the neck of one, then finish the other. But there might be a scuffle, or a scream. He couldn't have that either. He had to kill them both at once – silently, and bloodlessly. There was only one option: the Demon Arts of Death.

He crept into the hallway behind the strolling figures. At the same time he visualised a sequence of runes, invoking a technique known as the Snake Father's Knot.

Keeping the runes in his mind, he fixed his gaze on the shadowy ceiling above the two slaves. He beckoned to the darkness – and the darkness responded. From the pool of shadow above the two guards came a pair of serpents made from manifest darkness. Their forms were black as pitch, but obviously tangible. They hung from the ceiling, their bodies still joined to the darkness that had birthed them. Lazily they wriggled in the air, as though awaiting a purpose – or an instruction.

The hashishan focused his mind and gestured at the serpents. Each snake coiled itself into the likeness of a noose. Gesturing again, as if conducting some serpentine orchestra of death, the hashishan bid the snakes to descend.

The guards thrashed, but could not scream as the snakes wrapped around their necks and dragged them up into the air. Coils of solid darkness dug into their necks, cutting off not only their breath, but the flow of arterial blood to their heads. In shock they dropped their sabres to the ground. The weapons landed on the plush carpet with a muffled thud.

Still commanding the serpents with his gestures, still holding the runes in his mind, the hashishan advanced until he stood beside the struggling figures. They kicked and clawed at the serpents, but their efforts were futile; the Snake Father's Knot was stronger than any earthly rope.

It wasn't long until both men began to succumb to the perverse and gruesome effects of strangulation. One man had an obvious erection, while the other was pissing himself. Urine tricked down his leg onto the carpet. The hashishan drew back to avoid the splatter. Finally both men fouled their trousers – and grew utterly still.

The hashishan maintained the technique for a few moments longer, making sure the men were dead. Then he banished the runes from his mind. The serpents dissolved back into the shadows of the ceiling, dropping the dead men to the floor. They landed with a stifled thud, their arms and legs askew.

The hashishan took a deep breath and wiped the sweat from his brow. Using the Demon Arts was mentally and physically draining; he felt as if he'd just run a short marathon, whilst somehow playing chess with a master. He was tired – and yet, he had work to do.

One by one he dragged the corpses into the trophy room, holding his breath lest he smell the foulness in

their pants. From there he dragged them to the trapdoor, and hurled them down into the secret tunnels
under the villa. With his victims thus disposed of, the
hashishan returned to the trophy room, and waited in
the shadows once again. His job was to eliminate everyone who occupied the villa, and this seemed like a good
way to start.

***

Wena pulled away from Narseh's embrace. She was
tipsy from wine, but her necromantic senses were sharp
enough to detect the presence of death somewhere
nearby.

'What is it, my dear?' asked Narseh.

'I'm not sure,' she said. 'I thought I could feel something – something dying.'

Narseh shrugged. 'It's probably just a rat in the
walls. Don't trouble yourself. This is our special time,
remember?'

For a moment Wena remained stiff, her head swimming with worry. Then her lover crawled between her legs and laid his tongue on her lips, and she thought about nothing but pleasure.

***

The hashishan tipped another body through the trapdoor, then wiped his sweaty forehead. One by one he had slaughtered the guards on patrol. Desperate fingers had clawed at nooses; eyes had bulged; twitching bodies had shat themselves in spasms of death, until the reek of their foulness hung thick in the hall. Now there were no more patrols, just eight soiled bodies in the tunnel below.

The hashishan sat in the trophy room, feeling exhausted. The use of the Demon Arts was taxing indeed. He took some sweets from his pocket and gobbled them up, renewing his strength and satisfying his hunger. Then he took out his pipe. He figured he deserved another hit after his efforts. Besides, there was still a lot of work to be done, and he needed to maintain his murderous trance.

He sucked on the burning buds until nothing was left but a film of resin, then crept into the hallway. It was time to find the man from Alhazred. Where might he be? Where would the hashishan stay, if he were living at this villa? Probably somewhere unassuming, where no one would look. But his target was a different man, with different priorities. Ninia Zak had described him as flashy in appearance and flowery in speech. He fancied himself, and was fond of life's luxuries.

He's probably in the master bedroom, thought the hashishan.

And so he made his way there, scattering breadcrumbs of death in his wake as he slew what servants remained. He snapped a slave's neck as the man sat writing in a ledger; he strangled a sentry stationed in a doorway. He crept through the shadows with nary a sound, until he was peering round a corner at the entrance to the master bedroom.

Necromancy, he thought. *I knew it!*

For there, outside the door, were a pair of undead monsters wrapped in green linen.

The hashishan drew his sabre from its scabbard. He'd tangled with creatures like this in the past, and knew there was only one way to end them, short of slaying their master: total bodily dismemberment. He would have to chop them up. At least he needn't worry about bloodstains. The creatures were withered, and the blood in their veins was as dust.

He stepped into the corridor, raised his blade, and pictured a set of especially ragged-looking runes. Together they unlocked a technique which some called the Creeping Death, but which the hashishan's master had poetically referred to as 'Tzintillion's Stray Glance.'

He swung his sword through the air. A ripple of razor-sharp energy flew off the edge of the blade and severed the legs of the closest zombie. The creature went down, weeping dust from its wounds in lieu of blood. At once it began crawling towards him, while the other one charged, swinging its khopesh.

The hashishan parried – but only just. The creature had the horrid strength of death, and had almost broken his guard. He leapt back, avoiding another brutal swing. The creature was powerful, but lacking in finesse. He hacked through its wrist, and its hand hit the floor, still gripping the khopesh.

He didn't stop there. Swinging his blade in a series of elegant arcs, he hacked off its legs and its head, then finished it off with a disembowelling strike. Flowers and sawdust exploded from the lacerated abdomen.

Meanwhile the legless undead had crawled into range. It swung at his foot – but missed as the hashishan leapt back. He circled the zombie's prone form, hacking it to pieces as he went, as though he were chopping dry timber.

***

Wena's eyes flicked open. She'd fallen asleep in the aftermath of fucking, but something was pulling her awake. Instantly she knew what it was – her zombies were in trouble! She could feel their bodies coming apart, along with the spells that gave them a semblance of life.

A bolt of sobriety shot through her limbs. She was sleepy and tipsy no longer. She grabbed Narseh's shoulder and shook him awake. He peered at her groggily, and started to speak, but she clamped a hand over his mouth.

'We're under attack,' she whispered. 'My zombies are dying!'

Narseh's eyes widened in shock. From the hall outside came the muffled sound of chopping. Then the chopping stopped – and there was nothing but silence.

Narseh and Wena traded a terrified glance, then rose from the bed. Narseh seized his crescent-shaped dagger. Wena took her sickle from the nightstand. The two of them stood side-by-side, dressed only in their robes. They glanced around the chamber. The barred windows were high and narrow. The room's only exit was the door ahead of them, which just then flew open, admitting a man in black armed with a sabre. He stank of death and weed smoke.

'So you're the necromancer,' he said, fixing his eyes on Wena.

'The lady's occupation is none of your business,' said Narseh. 'And I'd thank you to leave, sir. This is private property.' He tried to make his voice sound as commanding as possible, but he couldn't hide the tremor of fear in his tone. The dagger shook in his grip.

'It sure is private property,' said the hashishan. 'But that doesn't mean it's yours.'

He advanced in a fighting stance. The curve of his blade was like a toothless smile on the face of death.

'Don't come any closer!' shouted Narseh, brandishing the dagger. He turned to Wena. 'Quick, my sweet – blast him with a lightning bolt!'

'I told you already I can't do that!' she hissed.

The hashishan stepped closer; Narseh gulped, then brandished the dagger again.

'Stay back!' he shouted. 'I'm warning you!'

The hashishan swung his sword twice. Two razor-sharp ripples of energy flew from the blade toward Wena and Narseh – and knocked the weapons from their hands with pinpoint precision.

Narseh raised his hands. 'Now let's just calm down here. Surely we can work this all out...'

Once again he tried to sound confident, but his voice had risen in pitch, and sounded almost girlish.

'There's nothing to be worked out,' said the hashishan. 'I've come here to kill you.'

'Then why did you disarm us? You could have cut our heads off with that trick. Clearly you want to make a bargain –'

'There can't be any blood,' said the hashishan as he drew even closer.

'Wait!' shouted Narseh. 'You're clearly a professional. Who was it that hired you? The Zaks? Whatever they're offering you I'll match it. I'll even add five percent!'

'Five percent?' repeated Wena. 'We'll double it!'

In spite of his terror, Narseh recoiled from such a

generous bribe.

'Don't listen to her,' he said. 'She's hysterical!'

The hashishan continued to advance.

'Alright,' said Narseh. 'Ten percent. But that's the absolute limit!'

Again the hashishan said nothing, and took another step forward.

'Fifteen percent,' said Narseh. 'You won't get any better than that!'

The hashishan drew closer still. Narseh took Wena's hand and leapt onto the bed, making a run for the opposite side of the room. The hashishan swung his blade, sending another crescent of razor-sharp force flying through the air. It sliced through a bedpost and slammed into the wall, slicing the marble itself. Dust erupted from the cut. Wena and Narseh froze in their tracks.

'Don't run,' said the hashishan. 'Or I'll cut you in half, blood or no blood, then shampoo the carpets.'

The two lovers glanced at one another in terror.

'Kneel on the floor,' said the hashishan. 'I'll make it quick.'

Still holding hands, Wena and Narseh knelt on the floor. Their interlocked fingers trembled. Standing before them, the hashishan removed a vial of black venom from his coat, followed by a solitary needle. Narseh saw it glitter in the moonlight, and began to weep.

'No,' he said, turning his gaze toward the ceiling. 'NO! It can't end like this. Candle King, I beseech you, don't snuff me yet! Please! Please, I'll to anything! I'll pile up the treasures on your altar. I'll send you slaves, concubines, armies of odalisques, spices, gemstones, mountains of tobacco, just don't snuff me out, not yet. I'm not rich enough. I'm too young to die. I've got so much to take. I've got so much to give! Please, please, don't snuff me OOOOOUUT!'

Narseh wept and rambled, wringing his hands and tearing at his beard.

Wena placed a hand on his shoulder. She was scared too, but still in control. Being a necromancer, she'd been surrounded by death all her life. Perhaps that's why she feared it less than he did. Then again, perhaps she was simply less craven. Either way she tried to comfort him, but he seemed to be off in some other reality.

'Begging won't save you,' said the hashishan. 'Stupid superstitions won't save you.'

'Then what will?' said Wena. 'Surely there's something.' She gestured around them. 'Just look at all this wealth! Let us live, and you can have it all. Even more, if you like. There's plenty to be had...'

'I know,' said the hashishan. 'I was planning to steal some, after I kill you.'

Wena clenched her teeth. There had to be something she could do to get out of this mess. The assassin was a businessman, surely. There had to be some kind a bargain she could make with him. But what? Narseh was the one who was good at bargaining, not her. He was the one who could persuade people, talk to people, change people's minds. But right now he was useless.

'Candle King, Candle King, save me!' he cried, as

snotty tears ran down his beard.

Wena felt her heart begin to sink as the hashishan removed the cork from his vial of black venom. She was almost ready to start wailing with her lover. Instead she took a breath, and steeled herself. Narseh was useless right now, so she had to take over his role. What would he do? What would he say, if he wasn't an incoherent mess?

The hashishan dipped the pin into the poison. Wena's heart hammered in terror. Then an idea shot straight into her brain, like a bat into a cavern at dusk.

'Wait!' she said.

The hashishan peered down with his sleepy eyes. 'Yes?'

'You're an assassin,' she said.

'No shit.'

'And your job's very dangerous, I bet.'

'Comes with the territory.'

'And I bet it gets gruelling, dealing out death day af-ter day. And it's not like you're fighting in wars, where

96

it's kill-or-be-killed, and your foes have a chance to fight back. You take them by surprise. Stab them in the back, kill them in their sleep. I'm sure it must play on your mind. That's why you're high right now, isn't it? To deaden your conscience. To tamp down your compassion...'

He glanced at her silently. She could tell she'd struck a nerve.

'What if I said you could take a break from all that?' she said. 'That you could still use your skills, but without any risk, and without having to hurt anyone at all?'

He peered at her in silence for a while, holding the needle.

'I'm listening,' he said.

Wena explained her scheme. The hashishan listened, but he was so hard to read, Wena couldn't tell if she were winning him over. His face was just so blank...

At length Wena was finished. For a time the hashishan remained silent, as if mulling things over. Wena's heart began to lift as he put away the poisoned needle

– then sank once again as he pulled out a dagger and grabbed Narseh by the beard.

'NO!' shouted Wena as the blade went slicing down.

***

'It's done,' said the hashishan.

Ninia sighed with relief, then smiled at the rest of the conspirators, all of whom were gathered in the room. The hashishan, who was seated at the same rickety chair he had used during his last visit, tossed something bloody and black on the table. Peering closer, Ninia saw it was the beard of the man from Alhazred, no doubt removed from his cadaver. She picked it up, feeling a sinister thrill as she held it. Then, with the air of someone who'd forgotten something important, she rushed to shut the doors and windows. As always, she didn't want anyone spying on their meeting.

'Tell me what happened,' she said, sitting across from the hashishan. 'Did you slaughter them all?'

The hashishan nodded as he loaded his pipe and

fired it up. Between each puff he spoke in great detail of the murders he'd committed and the deadly Demon Arts he'd used to commit them. Ninia listened intently, while the room became filled with clouds of potent smoke. It smelled somewhat different than last time. Even the buds looked different, being not black but crimson in colour.

Ninia paid it no mind. Nor did she mind getting a second-hand high – not when all her dreams were about to come true. She was finally about to get her hands on the old miser's money! She giggled to herself in delight.

I must be getting a bit stoned, she thought.

There was no doubt about it. Her body felt languid and strange. As she glanced around the room she saw the shadows of her relatives detach from their bodies and buzz with electric red light. Before she knew it she had fallen from her chair, and lay giggling uncontrollably. Her relatives fell down beside her, laughing like hyenas on the grubby kitchen floor.

The hashishan stood up, tapping the ash from his

pipe. His bloodshot eyes were cold. Ninia felt a surge of terror. Her body was numb. The fingers on her hands were curling up like the petals of dying flowers.

'What's...what's happening?' she managed to ask, between the fits of uncontrollable laughter.

The hashishan held up a crimson bud, much like the ones he had just smoked.

'This is Javasava Red,' he said. 'It's quite deadly. But I've been smoking a bit every day for the past seven years, so I'm immune to the effects. I doubt the same can be said for you.'

'But...but why?' stammered Ninia, even as her world became black.

'Because I'm a businessman. And I've had a better offer.'

'But what about honour? We had a deal!'

The hashishan repeated the mantra his master had so often spoken:

'Nothing is true. Everything is permitted.'

He turned and strode from the house. Wena and

Narseh were waiting outside. Narseh was touching the place where his beard had once been.

'Took me months to grow that out,' he grumbled.

Wena smiled at him. 'I think you'll look handsome clean-shaven.'

***

That night the Zak family mysteriously vanished. Searching their house, agents of the court found a vial of black venom, which prompted them to once again exhume the corpse of Muragar Zak. In his veins were found traces of the toxin. It was surmised that the Zaks had poisoned the old man, albeit inexpertly, which had caused him to fall into a death-like slumber, after which he had awoken for a time before succumbing to a heart attack. Warrants were issued for the arrest of the Zaks, and the miser's estate was handed to Narseh, who liquidated it promptly and departed the town, joined by a stranger with bloodshot eyes.

Chapter 7: The Plague of Undead

Shavran huddled in the hall with the others, listening in terror to the racket coming from outside.

Shavran was the mayor of Haresburough. A few minutes earlier he'd been going about his business as usual – collecting bribes, getting free blowjobs from hookers, and so-on – when a horde of zombies had poured into the streets, baying for blood. Some were bloated and fresh; others were old, with skin like withered paper unfurling from their bones.

Shavran had fled to the hall with the rest of the townsfolk. Presently the monsters were outside, groaning and banging on the door. The people within were shaking or screaming in terror, clutching the few meagre weapons they'd managed to get hold of. As the sounds of hunger and terror rose to an almighty pitch, a skeletal fist punched through the door, creating a hole through which the faces of the dead could be seen. There they were – a sea of sockets without eyes, lipless grins, rotting teeth eager to bite through living flesh.

'Fuck!' shouted Shavran. 'Save us! Somebody save us!'

In the next few moments his plea was miraculously answered.

First came the sound of galloping horses and the groaning of carriage wheels. Then the dead things began to fall, cut down by ripples of razor-sharp force till none were left standing. The air grew silent save for the whinnying of horses and the gasping of the people in the hall.

'You can come out now,' said a voice from outside.

Gingerly Shavran stepped up to the door and peered into the street. There, standing atop a hill of dismembered zombies was a man dressed in black, wielding a sabre. Behind him was a carriage. Sitting in the driver's seat was a man in a turban with a short growth of beard.

'Greetings fair citizens!' said Narseh. 'May I ask who's in charge here?'

'That would be me,' said Shavran, still reeling from the shock of the undead assault and this sudden reversal of fortune.

Narseh leapt down from the carriage and strode towards the hall. Gingerly he tiptoed past the bodies, avoiding the puddles of ooze and bits of mangled flesh. At length he reached the mayor, and held out his hand through the hole in the door. Shavran shook it limply, still trying to get over his shock.

'My name is Narseh Az-Pinah,' said the stranger. 'And this is my comrade, Zativa. We're professional zombie hunters. And we couldn't help but notice that your town's become the target of the Undead Curse.'

'The...the Undead Curse?' stammered Shavran.

'That's right,' said Narseh. 'The Undead Curse. Haven't you heard of it? It's sweeping the land like a wave, hopping from one unlucky town to another! I'm afraid this is just the beginning.' He gestured to the corpses on the ground. 'There will be many more monsters than this. Wave after flesh-hungry wave! But lucky for you, my friend and I can help. All we ask for is a small, meagre payment, simply to offset our operating costs. We'd do it for free, but a person has to eat, you know?'

'Of course,' said Shavran. 'We'll be happy to reward you.'

'Good, good,' said Narseh. 'Now, why don't you open that door, and you and I can have a talk about our fee structure?'

Epilogue: A Fantastic Tale

Some time later...

Narseh sat on a pillow in his palace, taking a drag from a jewel-studded hookah.

'And that,' he said, exhaling the smoke, 'was how I defeated the Great Undead Plague.'

'Amazing!' said one of the guests who'd come to listen to Narseh's fantastic tales. 'I almost can't believe it! Let me go over things again, just in case I've missed anything out. There you were, travelling through the Republic of Kurolow to pay homage at the graves of your many long-lost relatives, when you heard a man banging on the lid of his casket. You did the right thing and saved him, of course, after which he took you to the courthouse, willed you his entire estate, then suddenly dropped dead. You tried to have the will overturned, thinking it was very unfair that the poor man's descendants should be so disadvantaged. But in order to overturn the will, you had to stay in the town for some time, and go through the necessary motions. And not having anywhere to stay, you accepted an offer to reside in the old man's giant villa. But little did you know the whole thing was a sinister trap!

'Because the man in the coffin was a sorcerer. He wanted to escape from death by possessing a strong, virile body. But all of his descendants were feeble and weak. So he came back from the grave just long enough to will you his estate and trap you in his web. Being the site of his terrible magick, the villa was haunted by his spirit, which tried to possess you. Luckily your mind was too strong, and you managed to fight off his influence. The sorcerer, enraged, took possession of his granddaughter, and used her to hire a hashishan to murder you. But after a thrilling and incredible sword-fight, you managed to defeat the hashishan, and, rather than killing him, you graciously chose to spare his wretched life, after which he pledged to serve you faithfully forever. At that point the spirit, even more enraged, cast a terrible spell that unleashed undead hordes from the earth. Rampaging monsters began to roam the land, eating human flesh. Unable to sit back and watch, you took it upon yourself to send the foul monsters to the grave once again, facing terrible danger in the process.' The man paused, and took a breath. 'Have I listed all the details correctly?'

'Pretty much,' said Narseh. 'Although I must point out that slaughtering zombies is very expensive, and I didn't have the heart to ask for money from the poor, defenceless people whom I rescued. As a consequence, I'm afraid I used up a great deal of my capital in the endeavour. I still haven't quite recovered from the financial blow...'

Narseh stared sadly at the floor, which was inlaid with brilliant arrangements of lapis and turquoise.

'Such a sad world we live in,' said the guest, 'in which righteous men are so often left destitute, while liars and cheats are left to prosper without end. Well not this time, my friend! I for one would like to give you some gifts, not only to repay you for the tale of this thrilling adventure, but to offset all the hardships you've suffered whilst helping the unfortunate.'

'I should like you give you gifts as well,' said another of the guests.

'Me too!' said another.

The men stood up and clapped their hands, whereupon their slaves poured into the room, carrying wealth fit for an imperial procession – brocaded silks from the land of distant Leng, bearing the visage of the Saffron Sage; silver plate from the pornocracy of Thune, embossed with entrancing erotica; sacks of tobacco; pelts of exotic beasts; and various objects of wondrous appearance and incredible monetary value.

'You're too kind, gentlemen,' said Narseh, wiping his eyes. 'I fear I might weep. Perhaps you might leave me alone, so I don't make a fool of myself?'

The guests nodded graciously and departed the palace, whereupon a sly smile spread over Narseh's lips. The story had been bullshit, of course – well, mostly bullshit. He really had stopped a plague of undead, albeit one of his and Wena's creation. Luckily his audience had been chosen from the stupidest – and wealthiest – people in Alhazred.

He called to his slaves, who began to carry his new treasures to the vault. Narseh followed behind, passing the altar of the Candle King, which was empty of offerings as usual.

Soon he stood in his vault, staring at a sea of gleaming treasure which stretched from one wall to another. It was more than a man could spend in several lifetimes.

Narseh shook his head and sighed. He didn't have nearly enough! Especially not enough to finance his retirement in the afterlife. Soon he'd have to go back to work once again, and take another voyage across the wide Ozich Sea.

Narseh will return in more nefarious journeys!

About the Author

B.J. Swann is the incarnation of a cosmic demon who shall not be named. He has come to earth to usher in the Aeon of Chaos, an age of madness, mayhem, and pleasures undreamed of. He likes comic books, bubble tea, and boneless fried chicken.

Website: www.swannbedlam.com

Contact: bjswnn@gmail.com

www.swannbedlam.com

Also by B.J. Swann

The Unwithering Flower

Unbridled greed. Dark necromancy. Total Mayhem.

When Narseh the Slaver journeys to the infamous City of Whores, he thinks he's about to make a fortune trading in nubile human flesh. Instead he finds the city's population decimated by plague. His sordid mercantile venture looks utterly doomed – until a chance encounter with a beautiful sorceress changes everything. By combining her necromantic powers with his commercial know-how, the new allies use the site of the plague-ridden city to launch a money-making scheme so devious, so vile, so repulsive, that it will live on in infamy forever, and bring a storm of vengeance and bloodshed down upon their heads the likes of which the City of Whores has never seen.

Praise for *The Unwithering Flower*:

"One of the best Novellas I've ever read. Swann's vision is dark, unrelenting and full of black humour." - Simon McHardy, author of *Jaga's Bones* and *Mother Maggot*

"... this book has it all. A really fun read and I must say, a unique, original storyline." - River Dixon, author of *The Smell of Cedar* and *The Stories In Between*

"Undead prostitutes and necromancy... Really, what more does one need from a book!?" - Elizabeth Bedlam, author of *People who are Lost* and *Rabbit Skin Glue*

Also By B.J. Swann

Zhuulton of Zhuul and the Feast of the Centipede

Zhuulton of Zhuul has been given a quest. Unfortunately for her, it looks more like a creative suicide plan than a realistic goal. Before three days are up, she must travel to the heart of an inhospitable empire, infiltrate an impregnable palace, slaughter fifteen kings as they sit down to lunch, and defeat the great demon centipede before he ascends to the fourth dimension. If she doesn't, her best friend in the whole world will be eaten alive - with a side of mustard.

Luckily Zhuulton has the help of four shape-shifting demons, each with their own special power. One of them can sing. One of them can eat. One of them can smash things. And the fourth is filled with the dread essence of death itself.

Join Zhuulton and her magnificent companions for a madcap adventure crammed with sex, violence, and outright strangeness. Enter the Aeon of Chaos, where fantasy, horror, and humour collide!

'Gruesome, anarchic, and absurd. Like *Monty Python and the Holy Grail* meets Kentaro Miura's *Berserk*.' - Elizabeth Bedlam

Also by B.J. Swann

Zhuulton of Zhuul and the Conspiracy of Ravens

Fleeing a grisly battlefield, Zhuulton and Morning-star end up in the backwater city of Ravensfen, where spooky things are happening. A plague of suicide has gripped the land, and the only person with a smile on his face is the undertaker. People are hanging themselves, jumping off cliffs, even roasting themselves alive inside giant novelty ovens. An eerie presence seems to be driving the deaths. Ravens cluster on rooftops, the sound of creepy piping infects people's dreams, and many are the whispers of a deathly Kingdom where sorrow and pain will be forgotten forever.

To escape all this maudlin bollocks, Zhuulton embarks on a spree of juvenile mischief with a handsome young lad. And yet, wherever she goes, the darkness seems to follow. For in the cursed land of Ravensfen, all roads lead to the Kingdom of the dead, where the Raven Prince rules...